W9-CNH-361

1 2 3 4 5 6 7 8 9 10
❖
First Edition

RAINBOW FISH
SEAWEED SOUP

Text by Jodi Huelin & Namrata Tripathi

Illustrations by Benrei Huang

HarperFestival®
A Division of HarperCollins*Publishers*

"Good morning, class!" said

Miss Cuttle.

"Today you will begin a new project."

The little fish were excited.

What would it be?

"Each student will work with a
partner," Miss Cuttle explained.
"Each team will make seaweed soup.
The team whose soup tastes best
will win gold shells."

"Wow!" said Rusty.

To win gold shells each team

would have to work hard.

"Seaweed soup. Yum!" said Tug.

"I hope we get to work together,"
Rosie said to Rainbow Fish.
But Rosie did not get her wish.
Miss Cuttle announced the pairs.

"Rainbow Fish and Pearl

are a team," she said.

"Rosie will work with Angel."

Rosie was upset.

At recess, Rosie said,

"Rainbow Fish, let's play tag!"

"I can't today," he answered.

"Pearl and I want to plan our recipe."

What a goody two-fin,

Rosie thought.

Then she had an idea.

"Come on, Angel," she said.

"Let's get started on our project.

We're going to win gold shells!"

"Use the recipe we learned last week,"
Miss Cuttle explained after recess.
"You can add kelp, seaweed, and algae.
But be sure not to add too much
sea salt."

"I can't wait to get started!"
said Rosie.
Each team made their soup
after school.
The next day they would share
their creations in class.

The teams worked very hard.

They all followed the recipe carefully.

Each team added a little bit extra

of their favorite ingredient.

14

The next morning,

Rosie left for school without Pearl.

Rosie was confident.

Angel and I made the best

seaweed soup, she thought.

I am sure we'll win the contest!

"Rosie!" Pearl called out.

"Wait for me!"

Rosie stopped and waited.

"I'm going to win," Rosie told

her sister.

16

Pearl had been confident, too.

But now she wasn't so sure.

"Would you mind tasting my soup?"

asked Pearl.

"I brought extra ingredients along."

Rosie tried her sister's seaweed soup.

It was excellent!

It was better than the soup

Rosie and Angel made.

Oh no! thought Rosie.

I can't let Pearl and Rainbow Fish win.

"It needs sea salt," Rosie said.

"But I added one shell full,"

replied Pearl.

"Like the recipe said."

19

"One shell?" Rosie asked.

"You were supposed to add
four shells of sea salt!"

"Oh, I must have gotten the
recipe wrong," Pearl said.
She thanked her sister and
added more sea salt.
Then they swam off to school.

Inside the cave classroom,

the fish couldn't wait

for the contest to begin.

"Okay, class," said Miss Cuttle.

"Let's start!"

She tasted Rosie and Angel's

soup first.

"This is delicious!" she said.

Miss Cuttle tasted each team's

seaweed soup.

Rosie and Angel's soup

was still the best.

She tasted Rainbow Fish and

Pearl's soup last.

"Oooh!" she cried. "It's very salty."

"I added the right amount,"

said Pearl.

"Four shells full."

"But the recipe called for only
one shell full of sea salt,"
Miss Cuttle said.

"That's what I thought,"
Pearl explained.

"But Rosie told me I was wrong."

"Rosie, is that true?" asked

Miss Cuttle.

"Yes," Rosie confessed.

"I didn't want Pearl to win."

Rosie told the class that Pearl
and Rainbow Fish's soup
was the best.
"They deserve gold shells,
not me," Rosie said.

Rosie apologized to her sister.

Then she told Rainbow Fish
she was sorry.

They accepted Rosie's apology.

Miss Cuttle announced her decision.

"Angel, Pearl, and Rainbow Fish

win gold shells," she said.

They were all happy.

Rosie had to clean out

all the soup bowls.

And when she was done,

Rosie asked Pearl to show her

how to make such yummy soup.